First published in Belgium and Holland by Clavis Uitgeverij, Hasselt – Amsterdam, 2017
Copyright © 2017, Clavis Uitgeverij

English translation from the Dutch by Clavis Publishing Inc. New York
Copyright © 2017 for the English language edition: Clavis Publishing Inc. New York

Visit us on the web at www.clavisbooks.com

I Am Going to Bed written and illustrated by Liesbet Slegers
Original title: *Ik ga slapen*
Translated from the Dutch by Clavis Publishing

ISBN 978-1-60537-346-1

This book was printed in January 2017 at Wai Man Book Binding (China) Ltd. Flat A, 9/F., Phase 1,
Kwun Tong Industrial Centre, 472-484 Kwun Tong Road, Kwun Tong, Kowloon, H.K.

First Edition
10 9 8 7 6 5 4 3 2 1

I Am Going to Bed

Clavis
NEW YORK

Liesbet Slegers

I am playing with
Bear and Rabbit.
The wagon is the train.
I push it, shouting
"Choo-choo!" Goodbye, car!
Bye, blocks! Bye, ball!

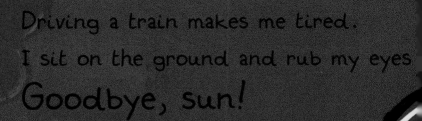

Driving a train makes me tired.
I sit on the ground and rub my eyes
Goodbye, sun!

I am taking a **bath**
with my ducky.
I take off my clothes.
What's in that bottle
next to the faucet?

Bubble bath!

It's fun to play with the bubbles.

I splish and splash.

There are bubbles on top

of my head!

I get out of the bathtub.

The floor is soaking wet! That's OK.

I dry myself with a towel.

I put on my **pajamas.**

I put my **slippers** on.

I'm all fresh and clean.

I grab a little book.

I like reading books and

I like looking at pictures.

Daddy will read to me.

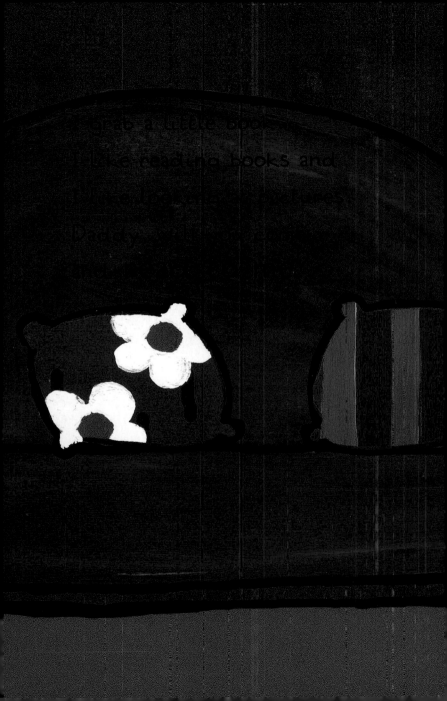

When I get tired,
I want my Panda Bear.
I can see my puppet and
the blocks and the ball and Rabbit.
Where are you, Panda Bear?

There you are!
My dear Panda Bear!
Have you been hiding from me,
you rascal?

My soft blanket is nice and warm.
"Sweet dreams, Little Bear!"
"Sweet dreams, Little Rabbit!"